Spartan +
FRIENDS
I0720874

210
CR
210

Raffy's Race
Colouring and Literacy Book

Consolidating phonics knowledge with extended decodable text.

Word Count
Approx. 419 words

Focus Phonics Sounds
ai – rain
ee – cheer
th – with
ch – charm
ar – spark
oo – zoom

High-Frequency Words
the, and, a, to, in, was, she, her, they, went,
had, with, for, as, on, it, of, by, that, his

Irregular Words
said, was, you, your, they, their, were, because, friend, through

Practice Words
affy, Spark, Remi, Pypah, Suki, motorbike, barrels, race, muddy, splash,
speed, helmet, cheer, timer, track, cousin, zoom, proud, smile, brave

Teacher Prep Before Reading

Phonics Warm-Up: Review ar and oo sounds (Spark, zoom)
using flashcards.

Vocabulary Support: Introduce or discuss, barrels, motorbike, race,
timer, cousin, muddy, splash, cheer.

Prediction Prompt: Ask: "Who do you think will win the race,
Raffy on her bike or Remi on her horse?"

Raffy loved to ride her motorbike,
zooming around was what she liked!
She'd race through fields, so fast,
so free, but horses? Nope!
They're not for me!

Her sister Remi loved her steed,
a black horse with bursts of speed.
Spark was shiny, strong, and sleek,
he sparkled bright, a rider's dream!

Their cousin Pypah grinned with glee,
Suki the pony trotted free.
Remi had owned her long ago,
now it's Pypah's turn to learn and grow.

Raffy rolled her eyes one day.
"I'd rather ride my bike," she'd say.
She zipped through tracks and muddy bogs,
while horses huffed through drifting fogs.

Remi set the barrels neat,
three striped drums for Spark's quick feet.
He trotted round with steady pace,
turning tight to win the race.

Raffy shouted, "That looks fun! Bet I can beat you,
Remi, one-on-one! She kicked her bike,
the engine cried, let's see who wins,
your horse or my ride!"

Remi grinned and called out loud,
"Challenge on!" she said so proud.
The timer beeped, she raced the track,
next was Raffy's turn, no turning back!
210
CR
210

Round the first, then round again,
they raced so fast across the pen.
Spark could turn with all his might,
and Remi won, but it was slight.

Raffy frowned but didn't quit,
"I'll learn those turns, I'll master it!"
Each day she'd practice near the rails,
with tighter loops and smaller trails.

Dust flew high and her engine roared,
her tyres spun fast, she wasn't bored.
Each lap was faster, smooth and bold,
she leaned right in, her grip took hold.

Then one bright day near the paddock gate,
Remi called, "Come on let's race!"
Pypah trotted over with Suki too,
they lined up ready and off they flew!

One by one they raced the drums,
galloping hooves and buzzing hums.
Laughter, cheering, timing scores,
the paddock rang, Raffy's engine roars!

Remi flew round fast and keen,
her turns were tight, smooth, and clean.
Then Raffy went, her heart beat loud,
she zipped around and felt so proud.
210
CR
210

She hugged the bends,
she braked just right.
Her motorbike leaned low and light,
the timer stopped a second spare!

Raffy gasped she'd won fair and square!
Remi smiled and gave a cheer.
"You beat us all, you're a legend that's clear!"
Spark neighed loud, and Suki too,
they all high-fived, below the sky so blue.

**Raffy grinned from ear to ear,
she loves her bike, that's crystal clear.
But horses? Hmm, they're not so bad,
with cheering friends, she's always glad!**

Activities (for after reading)

1. Re-read the story and circle words with igh pattern (**ligh**t, bright)

2. Find and <u>underline</u> all the words with ar (start)

3. Write 3 new sentences with oo words (zoom)

____

____

____

____

____

____

____

4. Would you prefer a motorbike or a horse? ___________________

5. Fill the gap: Her motorbike _____________ low and light.

Activities (for after reading)

6.Can you write a new verse, about how Raffy might have felt after losing the first race to her sister?

____

____

____

____

____

____

____

____

____

Activities (for after reading)

7. Write some words that rhyme with play.

____

____

8. What kind of race did Raffy and Remi compete in?

____

____

____

9. Who did you think would win the race? why?

____

____

____

____

Activities (for after reading)

0. Can you retell the important parts of the story?

____

____

1. What was your favourite part of story?

____

____

____

2. Can you draw the barrel racing set up?

Activities (for after reading)

13. What lesson did Raffy learn by the end of the story?

____

____

____

____

____

____

14. Complete the words with the missing sounds:

z___m

fl___t

ch___r

sn___t

l___p

15. Colour in all of the story pages.

Barrel Race Pattern

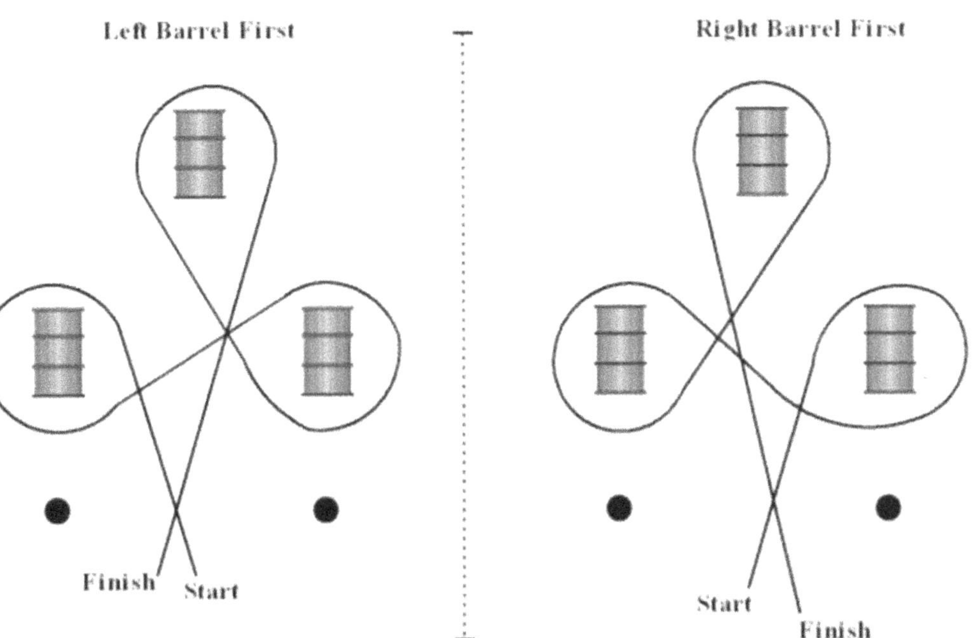

The standard barrel racing pattern requires specific
distances between the start line and the first barrel,
from the first to the second barrel,
and from the second to the third barrel.
The distances are typically as follows:

Barrel 1 to Barrel 2 - 90 meters
Barrel 1 to Barrel 3 - 105 meters
Barrel 2 to Barrel 3 - 105 meters

Spartan +
FRIENDS

www.ingramcontent.com/pod-product-compliance
Lightning Source LLC
Chambersburg PA
CBHW040548170726
48295CB00012B/632